For Kelly ♡

This is so you can
remember our second
trip to the Nutcracker.

Love, Mommy
Christmas 1980

THE NUTCRACKER

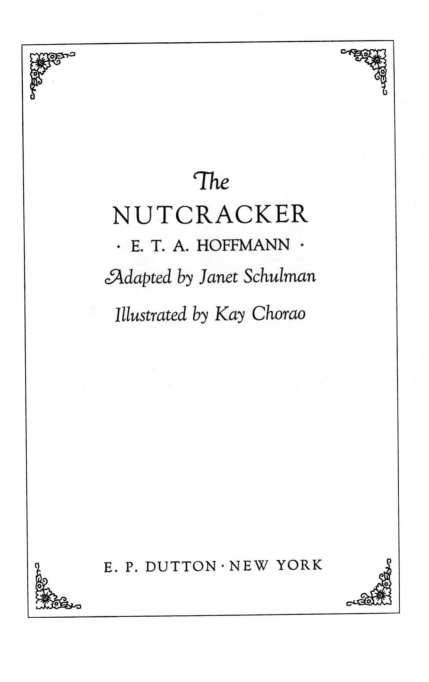

The
NUTCRACKER
· E. T. A. HOFFMANN ·

Adapted by Janet Schulman

Illustrated by Kay Chorao

E. P. DUTTON · NEW YORK

Library of Congress Cataloging in Publication Data

Schulman, Janet.   The nutcracker.

SUMMARY: After hearing how her toy nutcracker
got his ugly face, a little girl helps break the spell
and changes him into a handsome prince.
[1. Fairy tales]   I. Hoffmann, Ernst Theodor Amadeus,
1776–1822. Nussknacker und Mausekönig.
II. Chorao, Kay. III. Title
PZ8.S31276Nu 1979 [Fic] 79-11223 ISBN 0-525-36245-2

Published in the United States by E. P. Dutton, a Division
of Elsevier-Dutton Publishing Company, Inc., New York

Published simultaneously in Canada by Clarke,
Irwin & Company Limited, Toronto and Vancouver

Editor: Ann Durell   Designer: Riki Levinson

Printed in the U.S.A. First Edition 10 9 8 7 6 5 4 3 2 1

To Deborah Hautzig

NOW WAS FALLING gently on the
streets and people were hurrying home, their arms
filled with gaily wrapped packages. For it was Christmas Eve and, throughout Germany, children waited
in hushed expectation for night to arrive and with it
their gifts from the Christ Child.

Inside the home of Dr. Stahlbaum, Marie and her
older brother, Fritz, had stationed themselves at the

6

doors of the grand drawing room. They were under strict orders not to go into the room, but their mother had said nothing about peeking through the keyhole or the crack under the door.

"I can see Godpapa Drosselmeir moving about in there," whispered Fritz, nearly standing on his head.

"Oh, I wonder what pretty things he has made for us this time!" exclaimed Marie.

Their godfather was an unusual man in both appearance and accomplishments. Over his right eye he wore a black patch, and over his bald head he wore a frizzled white wig which he had made himself out of spun glass filaments. And he had a habit of moving his long arms and fluttery fingers and walking in such a way that he resembled a loosely strung marionette.

But strange as he was to behold, he was a delightful godfather. Never did he visit the Stahlbaums without

bringing Fritz and Marie some ingenious little windup toy that he had invented—a soldier that marched and saluted, or a little doll that clapped her hands and said "Mama," or a gilded bird that hopped about in its cage and sang a song. For Godfather Drosselmeir was a very clever man who understood springs and gears and all things mechanical.

His Christmas gift to the children was always some special work of art—too fine and ingenious, in fact, to be played with! So these special gifts were kept high up on the top shelves of the glass-fronted toy cupboard in the drawing room.

As it got darker and darker, Fritz and Marie sat closer and closer together, talking quietly about what they wanted most for Christmas. Marie wanted a new doll to keep her Miss Gertrude company. Fritz needed some cavalry soldiers to support his infantry and artillery men in battle.

All was dark and silent now in the house. The two children sat huddled together, absorbed in their own visions of what lay behind the drawing-room doors.

At last a silvery bell rang out and the doors of the drawing room flew open. A brilliance of light and color flooded the hall and the children cried, "Oh! Oh! How beautiful!"

What they saw was the most magnificent Christmas tree in the world. It was lit by hundreds of tiny candles that twinkled like stars. From the fragrant green branches hung all sorts of delicious things to eat—nuts and apples wrapped in silver foil, sugarplums, pink and yellow bonbons, star-shaped cookies and gingerbread boys, peppermint canes, and even little toy people made of candy—chocolate soldiers, marzipan ladies and gentlemen, and delicate shepherds and shepherdesses made out of sugar. There were tin trumpets and whistles and pretty glass balls dangling from the tree too, and spread out under it were so many gifts that the children didn't know what to look at first.

Marie clapped her hands in delight when she saw a large and beautiful doll, which she immediately christened Miss Claire. And Fritz kicked up his heels and danced like a jumping jack when he spotted an entire squadron of soldiers mounted on white horses.

Marie thought her prettiest gift was a silk dress with ribbons every color of the rainbow. Fritz decided that his favorite might be a chestnut horse, its regal head mounted to a long stick, on which he galloped around the room.

After all the other gifts were opened, Godpapa Drosselmeir's special gift was presented. From a huge

box came an exquisite palace with golden towers and many windows. When their godfather wound up all the keys, the palace suddenly came to life! A soldier marched out of his sentry box and paraded back and forth. Beautiful ladies and gentlemen with plumed hats and velvet robes strolled past the windows. And a Harlequin and Columbine danced in the courtyard. As the clockwork springs wound down, the little figures moved slower and slower, then jerked to a halt—until Drosselmeir wound them up again. They repeated their performance over and over.

It was a remarkable display, but after a while Fritz announced that he preferred his soldiers, who would do as he commanded them, and he proceeded to line them up for battle under the Christmas tree. Marie too grew tired of the dancing and parading little figures, but she did not want to hurt her godfather's feelings. So she continued watching until something under the tree caught her attention.

It was a little man made out of wood, standing there patiently waiting to be noticed. His legs were too short and his head was too large. He was wearing a commonplace green stocking cap and a short and narrow wooden cape that stuck out from his back. But the rest of his costume showed him to be a man of good taste. He was dressed like a military officer of high rank, in a lavender uniform trimmed with brass buttons and braid, and shiny black boots.

Marie fell in love with him at first sight. And the longer she studied him, the more clearly she saw what a sweet nature he had. His green eyes, though they stuck out a bit too prominently, beamed with kindness and loyalty, and his beard of white cotton drew attention to his cherry red lips, which smiled from ear to ear.

"Oh, Papa," cried Marie, "whose gift is that darling little man?"

"He belongs to the old and respected Nutcracker family," said her father. He popped a nut into the little man's mouth, pulled the wooden cape down, and—*knack, knack*—out came a neatly cracked shell and whole nut kernel.

"Since he has made such an impression on you," continued her father, "he shall be given over to your special care. But you must share his services with Fritz."

Marie was thrilled with the effortless and cheerful way he cracked the Christmas nuts. But Fritz called Nutcracker an ugly little fellow. He crammed the big-

gest and hardest walnuts he could find into the poor man's mouth, until finally—*crack, crack*—three teeth fell out of Nutcracker's mouth and his lower jaw wobbled like an old man's.

Marie snatched Nutcracker from her brother and cradled him in her arms.

"What's the good of a nutcracker who can't do his job? Hand him over," snorted Fritz.

Marie ran from her brother, crying bitterly. "Leave him alone, Fritz. He has done nothing to hurt you."

Their father separated the two quarreling children. "I have put Nutcracker in Marie's special care, which he seems to need just now, and nobody else has anything to say in the matter."

Marie's mother said that perhaps they had had too much Christmas and it was time for the party to end. Fritz put his soldiers on his shelf in the toy cupboard.

Marie found Nutcracker's lost teeth and bound up his jaw with a ribbon from her new dress. Godpapa Drosselmeir said good night to them all, and everyone went upstairs to bed except Marie, who begged to stay up a few minutes longer.

As SOON AS MARIE was alone in the drawing room, she examined Nutcracker's wounds.

"Oh, my darling little Nutcracker," she murmured. "Don't be sad. Tomorrow I'll have your teeth and jaw fixed. Godpapa Drosselmeir can do it."

But as she said the name *Drosselmeir,* Nutcracker seemed to come to life! Marie was frightened until, holding him toward the lamp, she was reassured by his kindly wooden face smiling at her.

"How silly of me to think that a doll can come alive," she said.

She tenderly tucked Nutcracker into her doll's bed and closed the cupboard door. She was about to go upstairs to bed herself, when soft rustlings and whisperings coming from every side of the room made her stop and listen.

Just then the grandfather clock started the wheezing and whirring that signaled its preparation for striking the hour. Marie glanced at the clock and was surprised to see that the gilt owl statue perched on top of the clock had thrust its head out and dropped a wing over the face of the clock. The whirring grew louder and louder until it formed distinct words of warning:

Clocks, clocks, clocks.

Whir, whir, whir.

The King of Mice

hears this purr.

Poom, poom, poom.

Strike his hour of doom.

Bells go chime.

Ring the fated time.

And then, *poom, poom* went the clock, striking twelve hollow notes. As Marie stared at the clock, the gilt owl seemed to melt away. And there, sitting on top of the clock was her godfather. His head was thrust owlishly forward, his coattails hung down like wings, and his arms were gesturing like a magician's.

"Why, Godpapa, whatever are you doing up there? You've given me a terrible fright," cried Marie.

But before she could say another word, there started the most extraordinary squeakings and scamperings and glitterings of tiny eyes, as score upon score of mice came squeezing through every chink and crack in the walls and baseboards. Then at Marie's very feet there was a sudden splitting and splintering of floorboard and the King of Mice appeared. He flashed a sword and glared at Marie with fourteen eyes—for he had seven hideous heads, each with a tiny golden crown.

The King of Mice hissed and piped his commands. His army of thousands drew up a line of battle and began advancing right up to the toy cupboard where Marie was crouched. She pressed against the cupboard door and her elbow shattered a pane of glass. The tinkling of the broken glass sent the mice squeaking and scampering in retreat. But from inside the cupboard Marie now heard a different noise.

It was the toys' call to arms! Behind the glass doors, soldiers, puppets, dolls, even the little candy people were running about. And Nutcracker was calling out:

Knack, knack, knack.
Stupid mouse pack.
All their skulls we'll crack.
Knack, knack, knack.

Drums beat, trumpets blared. Then out of the cupboard leapt Nutcracker, leading the toys to battle. At the sight of the little wooden commander, the army of mice regrouped and charged the army of toys.

Deafening sounds of rifles and artillery rang out. Boom, boom went the toy cannons, hurling sugarplums and nuts at the mice's front ranks. But no sooner would one rank fall, than a fresh rank appeared. The toys were being overwhelmed.

"Bring up the reserves!" commanded Nutcracker.

Gingerbread boys appeared from the cupboard. But the enemy quickly bit off their legs so that they clumsily tumbled about and simply got in the way.

Marie watched in horror as Nutcracker's small army was pushed farther and farther back by the horde of mice. Finally, three mice seized Nutcracker's sword.

"At last, I have you," squeaked the King of Mice.

Marie could stand it no longer. "Oh, my poor Nutcracker," she cried. She threw her left shoe as hard as she could, directly at the King of Mice.

Instantly the mice vanished and Marie's arm began throbbing with pain. As she sank to the floor, she heard the sad voice of Nutcracker say to her, "My dearest lady, you have saved my life, and I shall be eternally grateful. But it lies within your power to do even more for me."

WHEN MARIE AWOKE she was in her bed, her mother was bending over her, and the sun was shining through the frost-covered windows.

"Oh, Mama," said Marie, "there was a terrible battle between the mice and the toys."

Her mother looked at Marie anxiously. "It was just a bad dream, dear. I found you on the drawing-room floor shortly after midnight with a bad cut on your arm. Fritz's soldiers were scattered about and Nutcracker was lying on your arm. Now you must rest quietly today."

Marie sighed, realizing that it was quite impossible to convince a grown-up of what had happened last night. She lay quietly in bed all day until her godfather paid her a visit.

The moment he entered the room she sat up and cried, "Oh, Godpapa, how nasty you were! I saw you sitting on the clock and calling the King of Mice. Why didn't you help Nutcracker? Why didn't you help *me*?"

"Stuff and nonsense," said Drosselmeir gruffly as he twitched and jerked about. Then he sat on Marie's bed and said to her, quite gently, "Don't be angry with me because I didn't kill the King of Mice. That can't be managed quite yet. But to make up for it, I have something which I know will make you happy."

He pulled from his coattail pocket Marie's beloved Nutcracker, whose teeth and broken jaw he had fixed.

Marie hugged her godfather and said, "You are a nice godpapa after all!"

"But you must admit," said her godfather, "that Nutcracker is not what you could call handsome. Now I'll tell you how it was that ugliness came into his family and why Nutcracker and the King of Mice are enemies."

Long, long ago, in a small kingdom not far from Nuremberg, a beautiful princess named Pirlipat was born. The king was filled with joy, but the queen was anxious and uneasy, for she feared another queen who lived in the palace—the Queen of Mice, also known as Dame Mouserink. Dame Mouserink was angry at the king for having killed her seven sons.

"Just you wait," she had warned the queen. "I'll put a curse on your firstborn child."

And so the queen had Pirlipat's cradle guarded by six nurses and six cats. But one night all six nurses and all six cats dozed off. They woke with a start to the wails of the infant princess and saw Dame Mouserink leap from the cradle and disappear through a crack in the floor.

All six nurses rushed to the cradle, but what they saw inside made them turn back in horror. Instead of the beautiful little princess with perfectly formed features, there was a grotesque baby. Her glassy green eyes nearly popped out of her large head. From ear to ear stretched an ugly gash of a mouth.

The king placed the blame on the inventor from Nuremberg, whom he had hired to rid the palace of mice and who had, in fact, invented the world's first mousetrap to do the job. Christian Elias Drosselmeir was his name.

"Restore the princess to her original beauty," commanded the king, "or face death."

Now Drosselmeir was a very clever man but he was not a magician, so he went to the court astronomer for help. Together they consulted the stars and drew the princess's horoscope in endless detail. At last it was clear that her hideous enchantment would be broken only if she ate the kernel of the rare Crackatook nut, whose shell is so hard that a cannon could run over it without crushing it. Moreover, the spell would not be broken unless the Crackatook was crushed by a young man who had never shaved and had always worn boots.

Drosselmeir set out immediately in search of the Crackatook. But after fifteen years, during which he traveled the length and breadth of Asia and Africa, he concluded that the search was hopeless. He would have to return to the king and face the consequences.

When he neared his native city of Nuremberg, he decided to stop for a last visit with his brother who was a toymaker there.

"What luck you stopped to see me," cried the toymaker. "I have the Crackatook! And the young gentleman who can crack it!"

The toymaker produced from a jumble of boxes a nut of medium size that he had bought some years ago from a mysterious nutseller. Engraved on its shell was the word *Crackatook*. Then he called for his son who, though a fully grown man of eighteen years, had cheeks as rosy and smooth as a boy's. Young Drosselmeir had never shaved, and he had always worn boots, and his hobby was cracking nuts with his teeth, which were as strong as steel. Indeed, the young ladies of Nuremberg called him the handsome Nutcracker.

Old Drosselmeir and his nephew set off at once for the court of Pirlipat's father. She had grown even uglier than she had been before. The king was now desperate, and he promised that whoever disenchanted his daughter would win her hand in marriage.

When the princess saw young Drosselmeir she said, "Oh, he is so handsome. I do hope he will be the one to crack the nut."

The young man wasted no time. He put the Crackatook between his teeth, bit down hard and—*crack, crack*—shattered the shell into tiny bits.

The princess swallowed the kernel and—oh marvel of marvels—instantly she was transformed into a delicately beautiful young lady.

But just then Dame Mouserink squeezed through a

crack in the floor. Young Drosselmeir, quite by accident, turned and stepped squarely down upon her. Instantly he was transformed just as the princess had been fifteen years before.

Now *he* had big bulging goggle eyes, a wide gaping mouth, and a head much too large for his body. The unshaven down on his cheeks grew into a white cotton beard, and his cape turned into a wooden handle that stuck out of his back and controlled his lower jaw.

As Dame Mouserink lay dying on the floor, she squeaked:

> My newborn son with seven crown
> will bring the master cracker down.
> His mother's death he will repay.
> Beware, Nutcracker, that fated day.

Old Drosselmeir shook his head sadly at the sight of his transformed nephew, but he reminded the king of his promise.

To which Princess Pirlipat cried, "What! Marry that ugly Nutcracker! Send him away!"

So Nutcracker was banished from the kingdom, and with him his uncle. But before they left, the court astronomer consulted the stars. He foretold that Nutcracker could still be a prince but his appearance would not change again until he had killed the son of Dame Mouserink and won the love of a lady in spite of his ugliness.

"And that," said Marie's godfather, "is the story of why Nutcrackers are so ugly." Then he tucked her into bed and said good night.

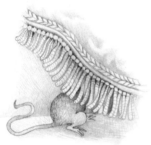

SLEEP WAS SLOW in coming to Marie
that night. "What an ungrateful creature that Princess
Pirlipat was," she whispered to her own Nutcracker.
"My dear Mr. Drosselmeir, you can always count on
my help when you need it."

Just as she was dozing off she heard a low rustling
and soft squeaking. She opened her eyes. There, standing on her bedside table, was the King of Mice!

"Give me your sugarplums, your bonbons and candy canes, or I'll chew up Nutcracker," he hissed.

Marie laid out her sweets for the horrid mouse, but the next night he returned with more demands.

"Give me your candy people or I'll make mince-meat of Nutcracker."

Marie loved her pretty little shepherds and shepherdesses and marzipan ladies and gentlemen. She did not want to part with them, but, for Nutcracker, she made the sacrifice. Yet the seven-headed mouse wanted still more.

The third night he boldly leapt upon her pillow and cheeped into her ear, "Hand over your books, your dresses and laces, or tremble with fear: Nutcracker's end is near."

Marie crept out of bed and went downstairs to the

toy cupboard. Tears were running down her cheeks and her voice was choked with sobs.

"Oh, my dear Mr. Drosselmeir," she said to Nutcracker, "what shall I do? Even if I give the King of Mice my beautiful picture books and my lovely new Christmas dress, he'll be back tomorrow night demanding something else. Soon I shan't have anything left to give him and he'll want to eat *me*!"

As she held him, she felt the wooden Nutcracker grow warmer and warmer in her hands. Then he began to move and, with some difficulty, to speak!

"My most precious Miss Stahlbaum, please—no more sacrifices for me. Just get me a sword and I can do the rest."

Then his voice died away and he became a lifeless wooden doll again.

Marie borrowed a sword from one of Fritz's soldiers

and fastened it to the little wooden man's waist. Then she went back to her bed.

She heard the clock strike midnight, and then she heard a rustling and a clanging coming from downstairs. Suddenly there was a shrill squeak and all was silent.

But at last Marie heard a gentle tapping at her door and a soft voice said, "Good news, Miss Stahlbaum."

The door opened and in walked a young man. Though he had no beard, Marie recognized him at once as Nutcracker. His head was still too large, and sticking out of his back was a wooden handle. But he was no longer a wooden doll. He was a living, breathing person.

He knelt beside Marie's bed and took from his arm seven golden bracelets. "Please accept these as a token of my gratitude," he said. "They were the crowns of the King of Mice. It was you who gave me the courage and strength to kill him. And now I should be most honored if you would follow me to my kingdom and share with me my hour of victory."

He took Marie's hand and led her down the hall and into the wooden wardrobe where he reached up the sleeve of Dr. Stahlbaum's fur coat and pulled down a little ladder.

"Why, I never saw that ladder before!" exclaimed Marie.

Nutcracker smiled down at her. "There are many things you've never seen that I should like to show you."

And he led her up the ladder and into the Land of Toys.

Snow was falling thickly, but it was not in the least

cold. When Marie caught a snowflake on her tongue, she was astonished to discover that it tasted just like sugar. Up ahead stood a pine forest that glittered and sparkled with gold and silver fruit and gave off the most delicious fragrance of orange and spices.

"This is Christmas Wood," said Nutcracker.

He clapped his hands and instantly there appeared a group of little shepherds and shepherdesses, so white and delicate that you would have thought they were made of sugar. Other little figures with reed flutes and pipes appeared from behind the trees; and as they played their sweet music, the shepherds and shepherdesses danced for Marie.

Nutcracker led Marie on, across the River of Lemonade, past Bonbonville and Gingerthorpe on the Honey River.

"We will avoid these towns," said Nutcracker, "as the people are quite short-tempered because they suffer so much from toothache.

"Let us sail across Lake Rosa to the great city in Toyland where my palace and court await me," said Nutcracker.

A swan-shaped boat made of glass and sparkling with gems of every color drew up to the shore for them. As they crossed the lake, Marie exclaimed, "Oh, look, each wave has the face of a pretty girl smiling up at us. I think it is Princess Pirlipat."

Nutcracker replied, "It is your own lovely face, dear Miss Stahlbaum," which made Marie feel quite suddenly shy and strangely embarrassed.

As they approached the shore, an inviting fragrance of all kinds of marmalade hung in the air. "That is the Grove of Jam," said Nutcracker.

"And who is that beautiful lady?" asked Marie.

In the grove, standing on a winding path made of baked sugar almonds and raisins, was an exquisite lady dressed in gossamer pink and white, and shimmering like a dewdrop. Marie could not stop looking at her.

"She is the Sugar Plum Fairy. In my absence she guards my kingdom and cares for my people," said Nutcracker.

The Sugar Plum Fairy approached them as if floating on air.

"Welcome home, dearest Prince," she said, curtseying gracefully.

Then Nutcracker told her about his battle with the King of Mice and how Marie had saved his life.

"I ask you," he concluded, "what princess can compare for a moment with Miss Stahlbaum in beauty,

loyalty, and goodness of every kind? The answer is none."

The Sugar Plum Fairy kissed Marie and said, "Now let all the kingdom welcome the excellent Miss Stahlbaum and rejoice at the victory of our prince."

They walked up the path to a large gate made of candy canes, behind which stood the dazzling white walls and towers of Marzipan Palace.

Crowded in the courtyard, waiting to welcome their prince, were all kinds of delightful people who were no bigger than Marie's dolls. There were Spanish gypsies, Swiss yodlers, Dutch maidens, Prussian officers, and people of every kind to be found in the world.

As Marie and Nutcracker passed through the gates, three Russian cossacks shouted, "Long live Prince Nutcracker!" They leapt in the air, clicked their boots together and danced, twirling faster and faster, like spinning tops.

"Come," said Nutcracker. "To the royal banquet."

He led Marie inside the palace to a magnificent crystal hall. The little golden tables and chairs reminded Marie of her own dollhouse furniture.

An old Chinese man waddled to the honored couple's throne, bearing a large pot of tea which two young ladies poured for them. Fluttering fans in front of their faces, they bowed, took mincing little steps backwards, and began an exotic dance from faraway China.

Course after course of delicious sweets—chocolate from Spain, Turkish delights, German gingersnaps, and all sorts of cakes and puddings—were brought to Marie and Nutcracker. And as Marie took the last bite of the last course, a veiled Arabian lady, with golden ankle bracelets that tinkled as she moved, brought tiny cups of thick, sweet coffee. Then she performed a slow, hypnotic dance.

Marie sank back in her throne in drowsy contentment and listened to the soft music coming from every corner of the hall. Slowly, one by one, hundreds of tiny flower people took their places for the Waltz of the Flowers.

Nutcracker smiled at Marie, his green eyes glowing with love. "Dearest Miss Stahlbaum, will you dance with me?"

As they glided across the marble floor, Marie whispered to Nutcracker, "Can it be? Is it true? I'm in Toyland dancing with you?"

Nutcracker gracefully led her in perfect time with

the music and smiled down at her, but he said nothing.

"I know this is not a dream," said Marie. "It is more like one of Godpapa Drosselmeir's beautiful creations."

"Your godpapa could never create anything like this," said Nutcracker stiffly. And then he swept her away to the waltz.

"Yes, it is true," thought Marie. "Everything and everyone here is so—so—I don't know—lovable and full of life. Not like Godpapa's mechanical things. I feel so cozy and at home here. I should like to stay forever."

The waltz music swelled around her and she gave herself to it and to the warm rosy feeling that uplifted her and seemed to make her float and rise higher and higher and higher. . . .

THE NEXT THING Marie knew she
was in her own familiar bed.

"Mama will say it was just a dream and Fritz will
say I am making it up," she sighed.

And so she never told anyone about the beautiful
sights she had seen or the happy feelings she had had
in the Land of Toys. Though long after she had
grown too old to play with dolls, she could often be

found in dreamy contemplation by the toy cupboard.

Then one day, not long before her sixteenth birthday, Marie gazed at the little wooden Nutcracker on his shelf and said, quite loud and clear, "Dear Mr. Drosselmeir, though some people think you are ugly, I love you dearly and always will."

Marie's godfather, who was repairing the clock, overheard her. "Stuff and nonsense," he said.

But as he spoke the drawing-room doors opened and a handsome young man entered. Suddenly her godfather looked happier than she had ever seen him. He jumped down from the clock and introduced the elegant young man as his nephew from Nuremberg. Young Drosselmeir bowed to Marie and presented her with a little collection of candy toys exactly like those the King of Mice had destroyed. And to Fritz he gave a real silver sword.

At dinner that evening Marie blushed as red as a rose at the sight of this charming young man cracking almonds for all of them. And she grew redder still when, after dinner, he asked her to accompany him to the toy cupboard.

As soon as they were alone he knelt before Marie and said, "My dear Marie, I have waited so long for this day. By saying that you love me, you have once more saved me. Now say that you will be my queen in the Land of Toys where I am now king."

Marie's parents gave their consent—and Godpapa Drosselmeir his blessings—to the marriage. To this day Marie and her handsome Nutcracker reign in a realm where all sorts of wonderful things happen for those who open their eyes and hearts to them.

JANET SCHULMAN's interest in writing this book began when she took her daughter, then about six, to the Tchaikovsky ballet. The child asked questions about the story that led her mother to the library. There she eventually turned to the original *The Nutcracker and the King of Mice,* written in 1816 by E. T. A. Hoffmann. In her retelling, she has included the Sugar Plum Fairy, a later addition.

KAY CHORAO says that "the *true* reason I illustrated this book was that Janet Schulman asked me to. But beyond that, drawing pictures for a classic fairy tale gave me the chance to expand a little. This is romantic fantasy, played against a formal nineteenth century German setting. To blend the reality of Marie and her setting with the exuberant fantasy of Nutcracker and his story was the challenge."